MW01089515

SPIKE, THE NOT SO NICE DINOSAUR

By Denise McCabe
Illustrated by Amadi Kumar

For Seán & Ava

Spike is a spinosaurus dinosaur who lives in Saurus Land. A long time ago he didn't have any friends because he was a bit mean to the other dinosaurs.

There was the time when Rex the tyrannosaurus and some other dinosaurs were having a picnic one day. Spike went over to them and asked if he could join them.

'I'm hungry, can I join in?' he asked.

'Of course you can,' replied Rex.

'Oh goodie,' Spike roared as he grabbed all the sandwiches up in one swoop and started munching away very loudly. He didn't leave any for the other dinosaurs. When he had finished he said, 'Ugh, that was icky, I did not like that!'

Rex looked at Spike with a sad face and said, 'That's not very nice, we all worked hard to arrange this picnic today. You're a big meanie, go away.'

Spike did not understand what that meant and he went away and looked elsewhere to play.

Another time Spike went to the Saurus playground. There were some dinosaurs playing with a ball. 'Oh, can I join in?' he asked.

'Of course you can,' said an iguanodon named Iggy.

'Oh goodie,' Spike roared as he grabbed the ball and started kicking it around.

After a while he announced, 'I don't like this game anymore and I'm tired now.' He then sat down on the ball and squashed it. All the dinosaurs looked at Spike with sad faces.

'Spike, that was a mean thing to do. That was our only ball. You're a big meanie, go away,' cried Iggy.

'The ball was broken anyway,' Spike lied as he walked off and looked for somewhere else to play.

He came to a big rock and sat down. 'I wonder why no one wants to play with me,' he thought. Just then Spike heard a voice, 'Spike, Spike, I know the answer.'

'Who...who said that, who's there?' cried Spike as he looked around.

A microraptor flew down in front of Spike. 'Hi Spike, my name is Mike and I'm here to help you make friends.'

'But they don't want to be my friend, they told me to go away,' said Spike.

'Spike, why do you think they told you to go away?'

'I don't know,' Spike sobbed.

'Do you remember the time at the picnic when you ate all the sandwiches and didn't think to share?'

'What's sharing?' Spike asked.

'Sharing is when you give something of yours to others or let other dinosaurs play with your toys.'

'Oh, I can try that. I have lots of toys at home that I could share,' said Spike.

'That's a good start,' replied Mike.

'Is there anything else I can do?' asked Spike.

'Well, there was also that time when you squashed Iggy's ball and didn't apologise,' said Mike.

'What's apologising?' Spike asked.

'Apologising is when you say sorry for making someone sad or hurt, even if you didn't mean it or it was an accident.'

'Oh, I didn't know I made Iggy sad,' gasped Spike. 'I must go and tell him I'm sorry.'

'Come with me and I will show you something first,' said Mike as he gently grasped Spike and with his super strength he swooped him up and flew them both up into the air and over Saurus Land.

Spike looked down at the dinosaurs playing and having fun. One dinosaur was hugging Rex.

'Spike, do you know why they like Rex?' Mike asked.

'I don't know,' replied Spike.

'He helped that dinosaur the other day when he fell down and hurt his head. He comforted him when he saw he was upset. He is always helping other dinosaurs. He shares his stuff and his love and the others follow his behaviour.'

Spike looked at Mike with a puzzled look.

'Come on, there's something else I want to show you,' said Mike.

Mike swooped up Spike and together they flew over Saurus Land again until they came over a house where Tricer the triceratops dinosaur lived.

She was in the garden talking to her friend Dippy the diplodocus who was upset because he had broken his friend's toy and he didn't know what to do.

'It's ok,' Tricer was saying. 'You just need to tell him the truth that it was an accident.'

'But what if he won't ever speak to me again?' sobbed Dippy.

'He is your friend and he will still love you because you were honest with him,' assured Tricer.

'Ok, I will try to do that,' said Dippy as he jumped away happily.

'What does honest mean?' asked Spike.

'Being honest is when you tell the truth. Even if you think you did a bad thing, or broke something accidently and you are afraid of telling that person because you think they might be mad. The person loves you and they would be happy that you were honest with them,' said Mike.

'Ok, I can try that,' Spike said. 'But maybe it's too late and the other dinosaurs won't want to talk to me now?'

'They will and I have an idea,' said Mike.

The next day, all the dinosaurs in Saurus Land received an invitation to go to a special meeting at Spike's place.

When they arrived, they saw that Spike had set up for a party. Spike stood in front of all the dinosaurs and announced, ‘Iggy, I am sorry for squashing your ball. Here, you can have my ball,’ and he handed Iggy his ball.

‘Thank you so much,’ said Iggy.

'Rex,' continued Spike, 'I have made a plate of sandwiches especially for you today.'

'Oh, they look like yummy sandwiches, thank you,' Rex chuckled.

'My friend Mike has taught me what sharing and caring is. Can I maybe have one more chance to show how I can be a friend?' Spike asked.

'Of course you can. You have shown us you want to be good and that's good enough for me and all the dinosaurs. Isn't that right?' Rex cheered to all the other dinosaurs.

Rex then took a sandwich but it fell down. He couldn't pick it up as his arms were too small to reach. Mike whispered into Spike's ear, 'This is your chance to be nice. You can help Rex pick up the sandwich.'

'Ok, I can do that,' said Spike as he went over and picked up the sandwich and gave it to Rex. Rex gave Spike a big hug.

Spike made lots of friends that day and learned all about the importance of what a little kindness, sharing and caring can mean to help others and to get along.

Did you know

Spinosaurus means 'spiny lizard' because it had large bony spines on its back. This was one of the largest meat eating dinosaurs. It was also the first dinosaur that was able to swim and more than likely it spent most of its life in the water. One of its favourite foods was fish.

Microraptor was one the few flying dinosaurs to have been completely covered with feathers, even their hands and feet. It also had Four Wings and occasionally gobbled up fish. It had claws on its forewings which were thought they were used to climb trees.

Diplodocus tails was around 45 feet long and it was one of the longest tails of any animal to walk the earth. Its head was less than 2 feet long and it had nostrils on the top of their head.

Tyrannosaurus Rex (T–Rex) could run up to 20 miles per hour and could cover 15 feet in one step! It had 50–60 teeth that were up to 9 inches long!

Triceratops had one of the largest heads of any land animal known and the skull could grow up to 7 feet!

Perspectivesaurus some say there was a dinosaur that was kind of like Mike that looked over the other dinosaurs and helped when they needed him. He may be still around to this day flying over the skies and helping those when we need him. Have a look up and see if you can spot him. Did you spot him anywhere in the book?

Can you spot five differences in the picture below?

Mike is playing Hide and Go Seek with this friends.
Can you help him find Rex, Dippy, Tricer and Spike?

SHADOW MATCH

Can you match the dinosaurs to their shadows?

Spike, Mike and Rex are having a race to see who can get to the plate of sandwiches first. Can you see who got there first?

Thank you for purchasing **Spike,The Not So Nice Dinosaur**.
If you enjoyed this and have a couple of moments to spare, it would be great if you can tell others by leaving a review on amazon.

I always appreciate feedback and comments so please contact me on denisekidsstories@gmail.com or come say hello on my blog www.kidsstoriesblog.com.

More books by Denise McCabe available on all Amazon sites

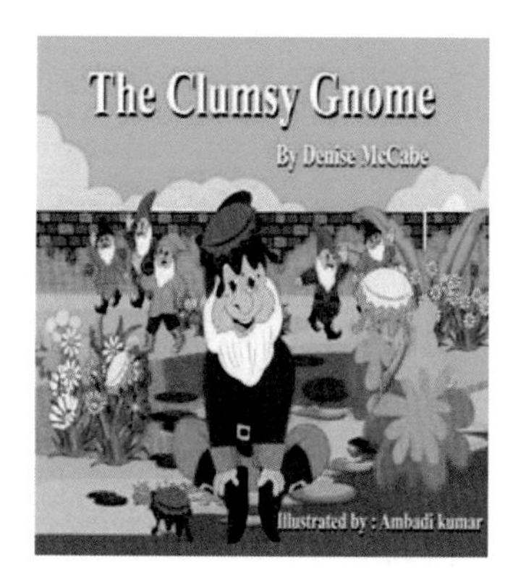

getBook.at/TheClumsyGnome

ISBN-13:978-1523937950

http://getbook.at/ClutterLand

ISBN-13: 978-1514376041

http://mybook.to/Gubble

ISBN-13: 978-1505866506

http://getbook.at/AdventuresofJoey

ISBN-13: 978-1508654841

Spot the difference

Hide and Go Seek

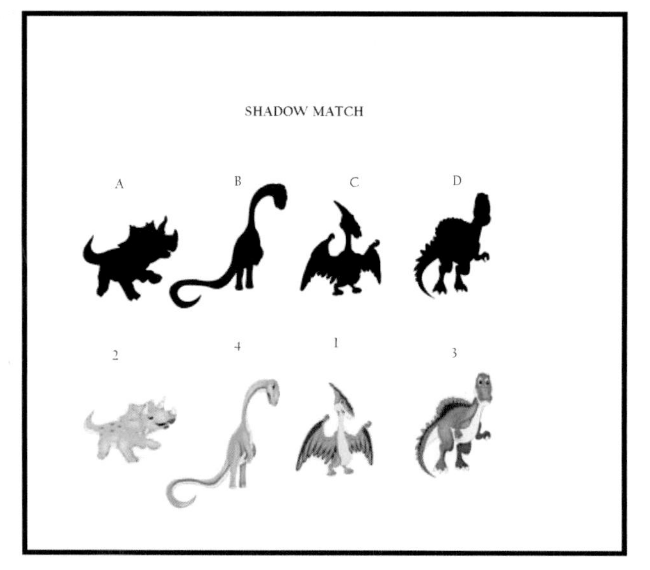
SHADOW MATCH
A
B
C
D
2
4
1
3

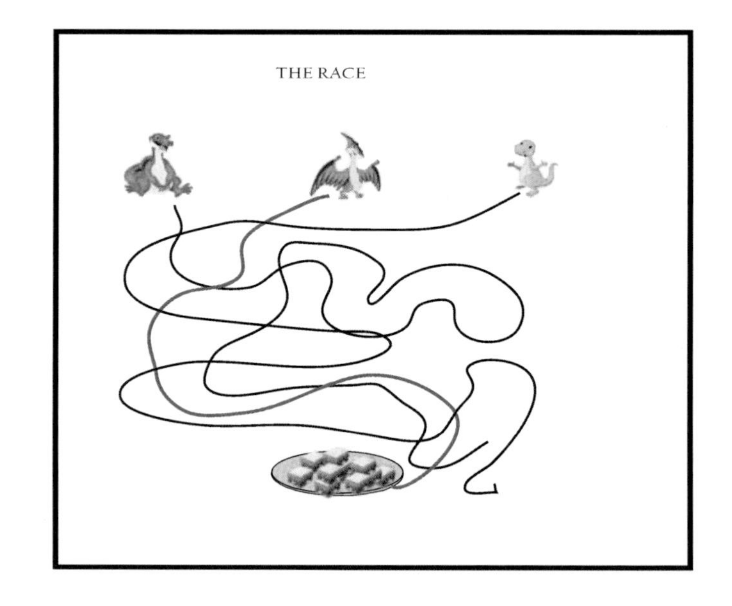
THE RACE

Made in the USA
Middletown, DE
07 September 2018